Cataloging-in-Publication Data has been applied for and may be obtained
from the Library of Congress.

ISBN 978-1-4197-3618-6

Copyright © 2017 De La Martinière Jeunesse, a division of La Martinière Group, Paris
Text and illustrations copyright © 2017 Christine Roussey
English translation © 2019 Harry N. Abrams, Inc.

Originally published in French in 2017 under the title *Mon lapin patate* by Éditions de la Martinière,
a division of La Martinière Groupe, Paris. This edition published in 2019 by Abrams Books for
Young Readers, an imprint of ABRAMS. All rights reserved.

Printed and bound in France
10 9 8 7 6 5 4 3 2 1

Abrams Books for Young Readers are available at special discounts when purchased in quantity
for premiums and promotions as well as fundraising or educational use. Special editions can also
be created to specification. For details, contact specialsales@abramsbooks.com
or the address below.

Abrams® is a registered trademark of Harry N. Abrams, Inc.

ABRAMS The Art of Books
195 Broadway, New York, NY 10007
abramsbooks.com

My Funny Bunny

CHRISTINE ROUSSEY

Abrams Books for Young Readers

NEW YORK

Today is my birthday.
I'm six years old. I'm so happy!
My favorite uncle is here,
and he put this big box in my lap—
my birthday present!
I'm sure it's a dwarf rabbit,
just like in my dreams.

I've dreamed of having a dwarf rabbit since forever. A mini dwarf rabbit as big as a kiwi—no bigger than that. So small I could hide him in my pocket when I ride my bicycle. So small he could sleep next to my pillow and sing me lullabies at bedtime.

A famous rabbit.

A rabbit world champion!

A rabbit that I would love with all my heart.

But when I opened the big box on my lap, here's what I discovered:

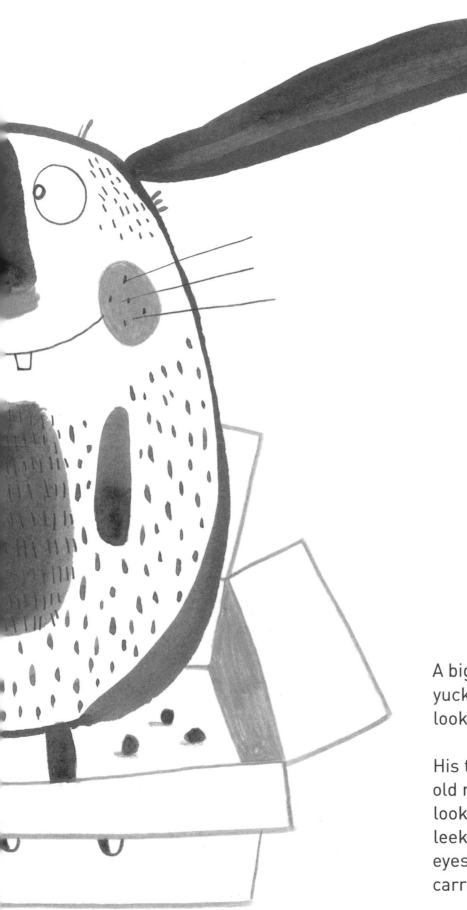

A big potato with patchy, yucky fur and whiskers that looked like wires.

His tail looked like an old rotten apple, his ears looked like two droopy leeks, and his two round eyes squinted atop his big, carrot-shaped nose.

I should have said thank you to my uncle for this silly-looking potato bunny, but instead I took the box and ran into my room. I put the box in the corner, and then I yelled as loud as I could. And then I yelled some more.

All that yelling didn't change anything.

When that funny-looking bunny raised his head out of the box to find out where he was, I told him that he had ruined my birthday. I told him I did not want him, and I did not love him, and that I would never love him!

I was very angry. I broke everything in my room.
I threw my collection of small treasures out the
window: goodbye acorns, pine cones, feathers,
and pebbles. I even destroyed my wooden castle.

And then I cried, sobbed, sniveled, and howled.

While I was crying, that
funny bunny jumped
out of the box and sat
next to me. He didn't do
anything. He was just
there. He was warm and
soft, and his whiskers
tickled my nose.
I started to calm down.

Funny Bunny crawled up on my lap. I rubbed him between his ears and gave him a carrot as a peace offering. He really liked that. While he was nibbling on it, he made chattering noises.
He seemed to be talking to me, but I couldn't understand what he was saying. It made me smile, and I think he was smiling, too.

Then he helped me fix my castle. It was a lot of work, but when we were done, it was even better than before!

Funny Bunny might look a lot like
a potato, but he made me laugh.
I was starting to like him.

I said to him, "I've been told that my temper tantrums are like big storms. I get worked up, then I explode, and then it goes away. Being angry makes me cry.
Do you ever cry, Funny Bunny?"

He didn't answer me, but he was right there with me.
It made me happy.

"Do you want to be my friend?" I asked him.
He didn't answer. I thought maybe he didn't understand.
But then he pooped, and I took that as a yes.

I told him I was sorry for being so mean.

And I thanked him for forgiving me.

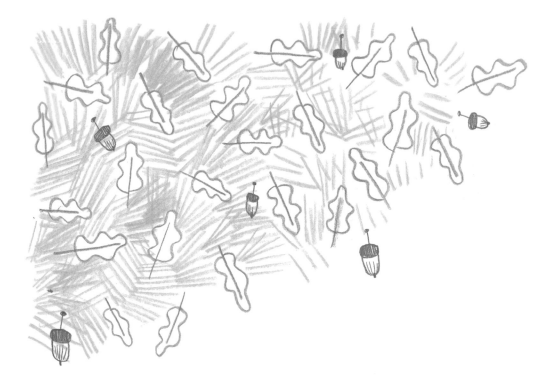

That's how,
on my sixth birthday,
my funny bunny and I became friends for life.